Brave Dave

The Makings of a Hero

By
Simon Woodward
Illustrated by Ralph Platt

Bloomington, IN  Milton Keynes, UK

AuthorHouse™
1663 Liberty Drive, Suite 200
Bloomington, IN 47403
www.authorhouse.com
Phone: 1-800-839-8640

AuthorHouse™ UK Ltd.
500 Avebury Boulevard
Central Milton Keynes, MK9 2BE
www.authorhouse.co.uk
Phone: 08001974150

This book is a work of fiction. People, places, events, and situations are the product of the author's imagination. Any resemblance to actual persons, living or dead, or historical events, is purely coincidental.

© 2006 Simon Woodward. All rights reserved.

No part of this book may be reproduced, stored in a retrieval system, or transmitted by any means without the written permission of the author.

First published by AuthorHouse 11/7/2006

ISBN: 1-4259-5996-2 (sc)

Printed in the United States of America
Bloomington, Indiana

This book is printed on acid-free paper.

For Molly and Tilly, my daughters. You're the best and always in my mind.

Special thanks go to, Ben Tuffs, Stephanie and Emily Paice, and Megan Owens for their enthusiasm and help.

But I also have to mention, without a doubt, Chris Debenham and Dave Judd, for their comments and for putting up with me.

Without their help and encouragement Brave Dave would have just remained a figment of my imagination and would have never appeared as someone everyone else could read about.

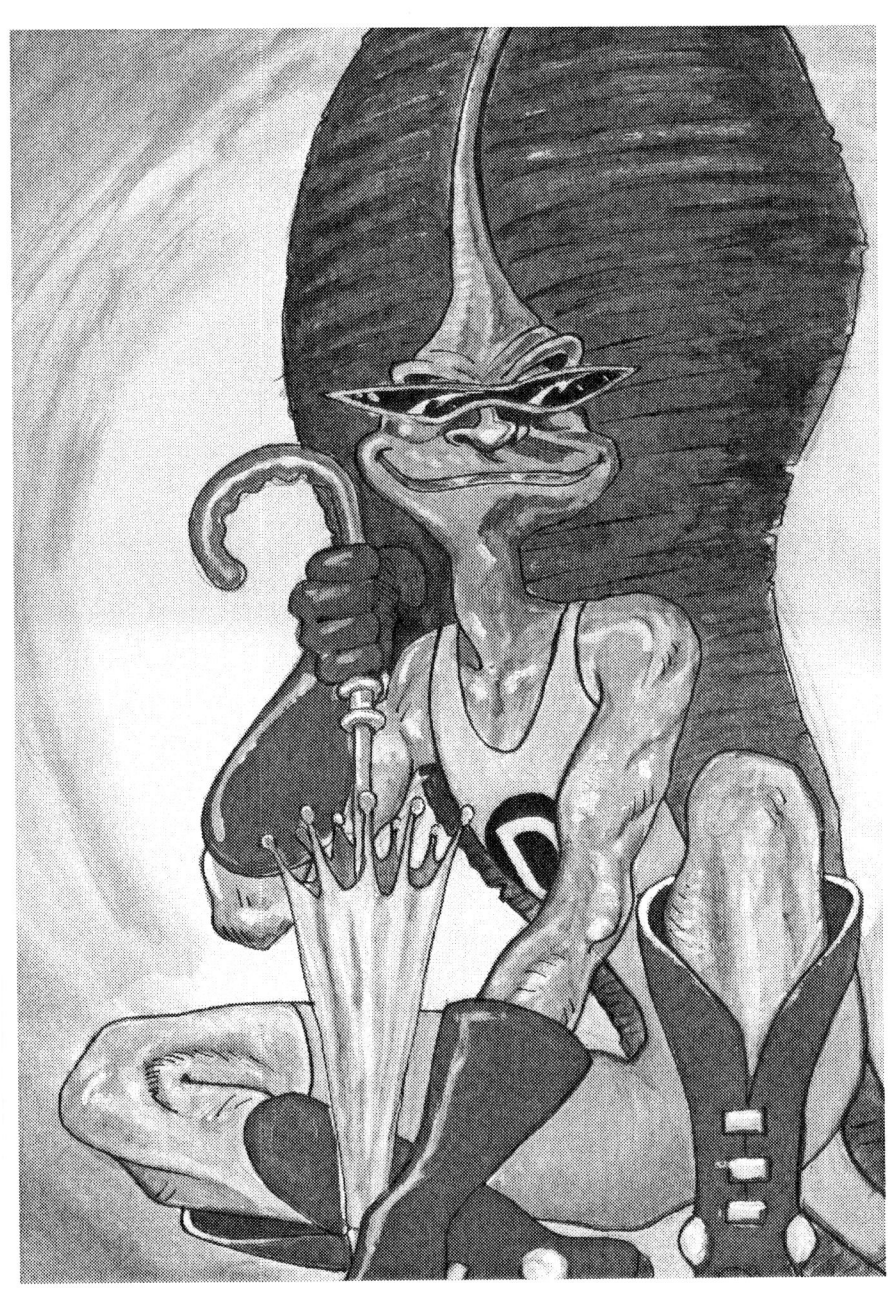

CHAPTER ONE

Announcement of the Practical Exam

"OK, you young Movitalls, you have completed your written exam paper."

There was silence in lecture hall 101 as the Movitalls waited for their results to be read out by the Headless Master, which would be a feat of genius for most people without a head, but this was Poltergeist University, so it was nothing unusual.

"I am very pleased," the Headless Master continued, "to say that this is the first year that...", Headless Master paused for effect, "YOU HAVE ALL PASSED." He boomed finally.

"Woooooo, wooooooo, wooooo." The Movitalls cheered in a low ghostly fashion.

Headless Master let the gathered students become silent before carrying on in a more serious tone.

"However, it is one thing to pass a written paper sitting in a lecture hall but it is totally something else to apply what you have learnt in the world of the living. And it is this, the practical exam, which you will have to pass so that you may attain gainful employment as a fully fledged poltergeist in the community of the living. My advice to you is; don't celebrate now but prepare. The day for the practical exam will be All Hallows Eve, and will last two days. Don't forget that the Masters from the Netherworld will be monitoring you during your practical, so no cheating."

The Headless Master of Poltergeist University let the point sink in.

"Ok, devil's luck to you all. Class dismissed."

The Movitalls got up and left the lecture hall thinking about what they had been told.

Brave Dave

CHAPTER TWO

From Lightning, A Life Is Born

It was Friday October 31st, Halloween in fact. Jonesy was rounding up his flock of swans to take them somewhere warmer for the winter. He was the boss.

You couldn't really call Jonesy your ordinary type of swan what with his beady little eyes, his hooked beak and huge talons in fact he was more of an eagle, a big one at that, but no-one had taken the time to explain this to him.

As spring, summer and autumn had packed their bags and left winter mooching about in what could only be described as a serious moody, Jonesy decided it was now time to get going and get his flock to Africa.

The weather was revolting. Extremely black clouds covered the early evening sky and the sun, just dipping below the horizon, spewed a few orange rays on to the grey and black cotton-wool underbelly of the clouds. Rain was streaming down in almost straight lines on to the lake making it seem as if the surface was boiling. Lightning was perpetually followed by huge thunderclaps and the wind was buffeting the lakeside hedgerow, behind which the swans now sheltered and where, during the summer, they had cooled off in the shade.

"Come on you horrible lot it's time we were going. It's now 18:20 hours.", ordered Jonesy over another particularly loud thunderclap.

"Ok flock, off we go." Jonesy swooshed his huge wings and leapt into the air. "Don't dawdle, follow me." He commanded.

Honking in excitement each of the swans in the flock took off to follow Jonesy southwards for the winter.

About 10 miles into their journey, with the rain still streaming out of the clouds and the thunder and lightning doing the thunder and lightning thing, one of Jonesy's larger and older feathers worked its way loose and started a long plunge towards the ground.

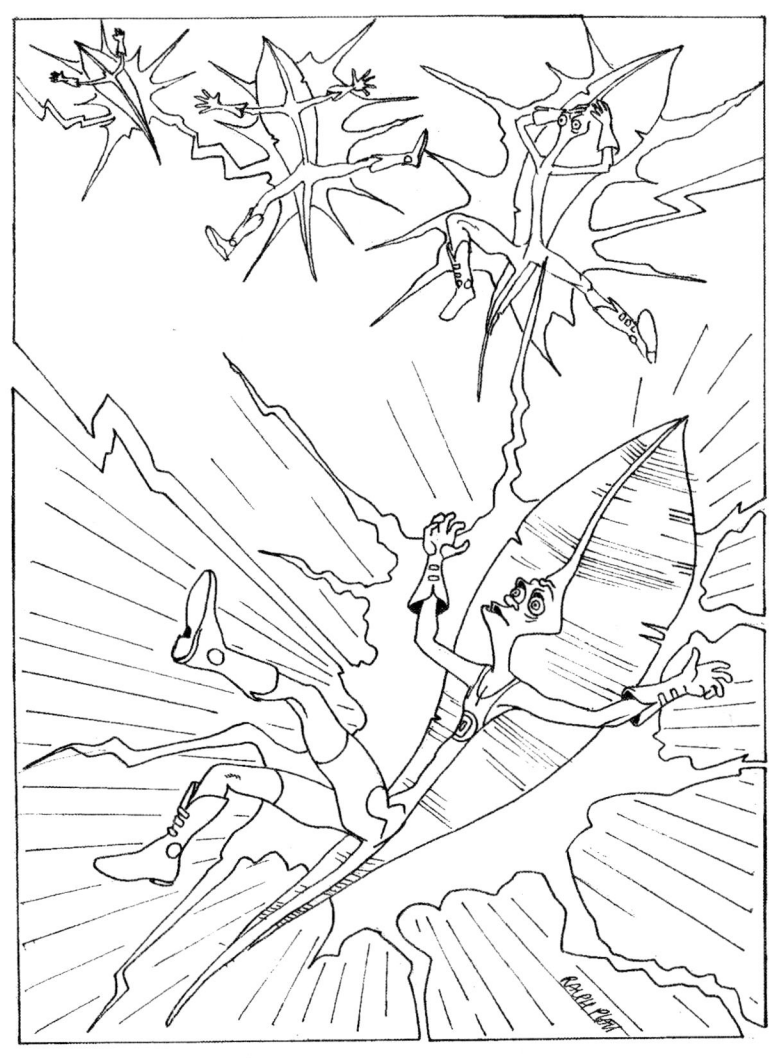

The time was now 8:14pm, 20:14 hours according to the 24 hour clock and a special time on Halloween. It was special because, by strange coincidence, 20:14 hours or "twenty fourteen hours" was an exact anagram of part of the sacred Halloween chant of the ancients, "Notnefurt-Ou-thyweers", which roughly translates, into English today, as "Without effort you will yowl when thighs grow under your ears".

Unfortunately the rest of the actual chant is lost to history, but accounts of it and its outcomes were widely written about at the time. It is in these accounts that other outcomes are indicated especially if you are hit by lightning.

The rain lashed the feather. Lightning struck it. Anyone seeing the feather in the fading brightness of the lightning flashes would be sure that somehow it had sprouted its own arms.

Another strike of lightning hit the feather. In most cases this would be viewed as very unlucky, but as it was during the special time the worst that happened was that a couple of legs grew out from its base.

Flash.

The feather was hit again; a pair of beady black eyes popped open and looked around rather startled.

Flash.

"Ow." Yelped the feather as it was hit for the fourth time and gained a mouth

"Oooo." The feather continued putting its newly grown hands into its newly gained pockets and finding out that it could not reach the bottom of them.

The feather rolled over in the air on to its front to have a look through its new eyes at where it was going.

Oh no, the feather thought as it saw the gooey, sticky, wet and smelly mud it was about to collide with.

CHAPTER THREE

Tariq and the Strange Utterances.

THWOP

Tariq almost jumped out of his skin, which was quite amazing for him as he had a very thick shell surrounding it.

What on earth was that noise? Tariq wondered gingerly detaching himself from the ceiling of his hutch.

Tariq was an unfortunate beast; unlike the rest of his kin he was wide-awake. He ought to be sound asleep and be sound asleep for at least the next five months, six if he was lucky and this was, if his friends were to be believed. But this wasn't to be as Tariq was an insomniac, he just couldn't sleep.

Once a year, in April, all of his mates would meet up at the "Tall Story Tortoise Talkathon" to catch up on old times, have a good laugh at the old Aesop yarn about the hare, and make general chit chat about the dreams they had had over the last six months.

Tariq was not quite sure what a dream was, but he was certain that he would probably like to have one.

Once it was mentioned, at the Talkathon, that he may have insomnia and this was probably why he didn't dream, but Tariq thought it was just a word his mates had made up to tease him.

Tariq the tortoise poked his head out of the hutch, What horrible weather, he thought. Squinting through the rain and the dark he saw something lying in the mud at the end of his chicken wire pen. It seemed to be attempting to unstick itself from the goo.

Ahh! So that's what the noise was, Tariq mused. *But what is it?*

Tariq shut his hutch door and went to his Ottoman chest which was a very old deep wooden box with a heavy lid. He opened the lid and pulled out his trusty yellow umbrella, his sunglasses, an old bin liner and a dictionary then shoved them all but the umbrella into his canvas satchel which he slung over his shoulder. Now he was fully prepared, he was ready to go and investigate further. Just before leaving his hutch Tariq put on his trusty deerstalker hat to protect himself from the pouring rain.

Edging his way down the ramp, the ramp which lead up to his hutch, he carefully and quietly put his bin liner on the ground. He looked towards the end of his pen which was some five metres away.

The thing that had landed there didn't look like it was going to make any attempt to move towards him, although it was jittering like a rather large flea would if it had somehow become stuck in the centre of a strawberry jelly.

Jumping on to the bin liner Tariq thrust the top of the up turned umbrella into the ground and pushed himself forward, punting over the mud towards the shivering shape. As he got closer he dragged the top of his umbrella backwards through the mud to slow himself down.

He didn't like this, didn't like it one bit. Tariq removed the sunglasses from his satchel and placed them on his belt.

The shape had freed itself slightly and was now attempting to sit up.

"Halt. Who sits there?" Tariq said pretending to be heroic, ever readying his sunglasses; sunglasses were always a useful tool in this type of situation.

"hmmmerr", the shape uttered unexpectedly. Tariq, for the second time this evening tried to leap out of his skin. He really hadn't expected this thing in the mud to make any kind of noise at all.

Fortunately his shell saved him once more. Tariq was certain that one day his shell would say, "Oh, go on then", and just let his skin go, but it wasn't going to be this night.

"Errrr. What? Pardon?" Tariq hadn't quite got the knack of interrogating shapes of unknown origin but he was learning fast.

"hermave", moaned the shape.

Tariq reached for his satchel and pulled out Colin's Dictionary of Unknown Vocabulary, 'Hermave', Tariq pondered, "Is that with one 'r' or two?"

"hime ave", the shape said more firmly.

"Sorry, you got me there as well. Can't find 'hermave' or 'herrmave' and neither can I find 'hime ave'. Can you mime it?"

With this said the shape struggled, lurched, wobbled, and finally pulled itself up to its entire height of around sixty centimetres.

"Whoa!", said Tariq taken aback, almost leaping from his skin once more.

"If you do that once more", Tariq's shell bemoaned, "I will stay in the hutch for the next five years or until you get so bored you decide to try eating your furniture with marmalade on, so that I will not have to suffer these bashings every time your lily-livered head decides to take fright at anything it feels like. OK?"

After all the years Tariq had spent on his own, during the winter months wide awake, he had taken to talking to his shell just to pass the time. Now she had become almost real, someone he could chat to and unfortunately someone he had lots of disagreements with.

Tremendous, thought Tariq, "OK,…sorry".

Next the shape, which now looked like a rather large flattened, brown, gloopy banana, started gesturing towards its chest. Following this movement it then vigorously gestured towards Tariq.

The flat brown gloopy banana shape then spluttered, "Ou r ou?"

Tariq took his up-turned umbrella, stuck it into the mud and punted backwards to a safer distance from the unknown shape, all the while making sure that he stayed within his skin. Tariq didn't exactly like the thought of having to eat marmalade for the next five years.

As the chance arrived he quickly thumbed through Colin's Dictionary of Unknown Vocabulary only to find that, once again, these utterances where truly unknown unknowns to Colin. Tariq wondered why he had ever borrowed Colin's dictionary in the first place. It was truly useless. He made a mental note to give it back the next time he bumped into Colin.

Looking up from the dictionary he discovered, to his shock and horror, that the gloopy brown shape was making its way towards him across the wet slurry that was the end of his pen.

Mentally instructing the head of his liver not to turn into a lily he grabbed the sunglasses from his belt.

Wait 'til you see the whites of its eyes, whites of its eyes, he instructed himself,

"It hasn't got any whites of its eyes." Tariq's shell piped up.

"Well that's just tremendous. Thanks for your help Shell. Will you now, please, shut up".

NO WHITES OF EYES, Tariq shouted to himself in his head, *Argh!* He continued, *What do I do now? I know, I'll wait to see the pinks of its palms.*

"They're brown". Tariq's shell continued.

"Right, OK, I'll wait 'til I see the browns of its palms. Now just be quiet".

Tariq stood there, on his bin liner raft, knees quivering, umbrella in one hand and the sunglasses in the other.

Browns of its palms, browns of its palms, he told himself again and again.

The globby brown mass was now staggering slowly towards Tariq, every now and then lurching from one side to the other just catching its balance each time.

Get ready, get ready, any minute now, Tariq thought trying to control the ever-increasing urge to propel himself backwards as fast as he could, away from the brown thing.

It was now within distance. Tariq took aim and threw the sunglasses at the strange shape as if he was throwing a Frisbee.

Round and round the sunglasses span, flying through the air towards their intended target.

Thwack, the sunglasses attached themselves just about where the brown shape's eyes ought to be, if it, in fact, had any. It was too dark to tell if it was a direct hit.

The force of the sunglasses spun the gloopy brown shape around. The shape threw its arms up in the air to steady itself to no avail. It had just a second to wonder why everything had gone completely black before the force of the glasses unbalanced it completely and pushed it over on to its back, into the sticky mud. The shape was now where it had started from.

Tariq saw his opportunity. Quickly he turned around and used the up-turned umbrella to start punting back up the pen, across the surface of the goo, towards his hutch as fast as he could. The greater the distance Tariq put between himself and that gloopy brown thing the better. He started to relax slightly.

Only three more metres to go. He made another huge punt and then another. Something was wrong, very wrong, he was slowing down. Tariq attempted another punt which felt a little too easy for his liking. He looked to where his umbrella was meant to be.

Uh oh!, he thought. His hands were empty. Tariq looked back down his pen. In the gloom he could make out, some two metres away, some two metres towards that gloopy brown flat banana like object, a grimy yellow umbrella sticking up out of the mud.

Oh no. I'm marooned, I can't go across the mud without the bin liner because I'll sink and stick and die. Oh no. I'm not going anywhere because the umbrella is stuck. And surely, very soon, that awful gloopy brown flat banana will certainly realise why it's so dark now. And when that happens it will seek me out, track me down and who knows what it'll do then. Oh, oh, oh. Tariq moaned to himself.

He was almost ready to leap out of his skin again, but realising he would still be stuck in the same place he thought better of it.

"Paddle." Said Shell.

"What?"

"Just paddle." Shell re-iterated.

"Welllll it's about time too. This is certainly a turn up for the books. Shell actually saying something useful. Well I'll be. And just for your information, that was exactly what I was going to do anyway." Tariq said indignantly.

"Didn't sound like it to me. 'I'll sink and stick and die'", Shell taunted.

Ignoring Shell Tariq got down on his stomach, reached over the side of the bin liner and started paddling as fast as he could. He looked back over his shoulder, nothing was moving apart from the rain coming out of the sky, the trees blowing in the wind and his bin liner, which was gradually picking up speed over the mud, moving towards the ramp and his lovely warm hutch. Tariq glanced back once more and was worried; there was no sign of the gloopy brown thing.

Tremendous, he thought.

CHAPTER FOUR

Voices, clips and mud.

Dave didn't know what to make of the situation. This was the first time he had been away from his fellow feathers and somehow he had ended up with a stinging clip around the face, a total blackout and his mouth filled with wet, gooey mud. He was used to being covered with dry mud in the summer, whilst taking a bath, but had never had to have a clip around the face to do that.

Must be the rain, he thought. The mud was not strictly unpleasant, but it did make speaking rather difficult, and moving; well that was almost an impossibility.

In this dismal weather, in the dark, he hadn't been able to quite make out the shape that had been shouting at him.

Apart from the clip round the face, his mouth being filled with mud, and the fact that he was stuck in it on his back, he was certain the shape that had been yelling at him was basically friendly. Dave pushed himself up on to his elbows.

However, he started thinking to himself again, *that's the last time I judge a book by its cover especially when I can't see it in the dark. So from now on I can judge a book by its cover only when I can actually see it before I make any judgement.*

Happy with this reasoning, Dave flopped back into the goo to collect his thoughts.

CHAPTER FIVE

Logical?

"Yesssss, huzzar, most spondicious", Tariq said aloud, pretending to himself that all was OK.

He had made it back to the bottom of the ramp and was very nearly back in his pleasantly warm hutch. Jumping off the bin liner he ran up the ramp into his hutch as fast as he could. Heart a pounding he slammed his hutch door shut and bolted it.

Tremendous. He thought .

"Chicken." Tariq's shell exclaimed for all the world to hear.

"IIII'mmmm soooo glad you're back to your old self Shell. I wouldn't have known what to do if you hadn't been." Tariq said sarcastically.

The next things he did in this situation were going to be very important. Something had landed in his pen, without permission, and he was going to have to deal with this.

Being a gifted insomniac tortoise, as his friends always called him, (actually they just called him insomniac, he'd decided to add the gifted bit), meant that he was entitled to have his own way to sort out the problems he had to face every now and then.

It was time to make sense of everything that had happened since the big thwop and the moments after he had stuck his head out of the hutch.

He got out his mental notebook and read through the points that he had made earlier.

1. Big thwop,
2. Wet head
3. Gooey mud
4. Peculiar gloopy thing
5. Frisbee glasses

Tariq was certain there was something he had left out. If only he could just grasp that part then, perhaps, he could make sense of the whole situation. He racked his brains struggling to think of the missing note, the part that could reveal all the hidden mysteries that were yet to be revealed.

Only one more thing, he thought to himself. *YES, I've got it, 5B – heroic return.*

Now he had all the information in place it was time to work out what it meant.

If 1 lead to 2 and 2 indicated 3 then 3 meant there was 1 which also meant there was 4 and as there was 4 then there must have been 5, and 5B of course.

"Tremendous!."

"Great." Said Shell, "So you have worked out that you have read your notes based on your experiences. FANTASTIC."

"Shell you just do not understand the meaning of this. There is something out there that is trying to hide and this means that it doesn't want to be seen and this fact alone tells me that it won't be bothering me any longer."

"And?" snapped Shell

"And, I can forget about it. This evening's events are over."

"Well", Shell started hesitantly, "I am certainly happy that you have made that clear to me now. NOT."

CHAPTER SIX

Mud and Presents.

Dave stood up once again trying to shake off all the dirt he had accumulated during his journey. He reached for his eyes and pulled off the odd object that had become wedged on his face after meeting the strange mud gliding individual, albeit at a distance.

He examined the object, Ray-Ban!, he saw from the label. Dave was pretty impressed.

This must be a greeting present. Not sure why I should have one but obviously they want to meet me. And why not? were his subsequent thoughts.

Dave had never assumed that he would be anything more than just a friend to anyone he met. His current situation was a little bit more complicated to comprehend than usual.

For a start, why would anyone want to give him a present so forcefully? Perhaps they wanted to be real close friends?

These thoughts didn't fit with the fact that the 'real close friend' had disappeared into the hutch so fast after giving him the present.

No worries, Dave thought, *perhaps they're just a little bit shy.*

He was well aware that, on an individual basis, everyone had their own way of making friends. He still had to admit to himself that this way was a bit more extreme than most!

Dave went on to shake off the extra wet dirt by performing the secret wet dirt removal dance. Just before performing the dance he had a quick look round. It was very important that before starting this routine there were no on lookers as this was the 'sacred wet dirt removal' routine that was only to be known to his kind.

After a few side steps, a back bend and a little shimmy he was clear of the worst of the wet dirt. Now it was time to make his way to the hutch, the hutch of the real friend, and introduce himself.

Dave stomped his way up the pen not bothering about the mud. He was more than capable of tackling this level of stickiness, or so he assumed. Abruptly he came to a halt. He was now concerned. Dave was not able to shift his legs in any direction; he was now up to his waist in the goo. It was obvious that without any help he was going nowhere. He tried shifting his legs once more only to find, to his dismay, that he just sunk further into the mud.

Dave looked around in desperation and caught a glimpse of a yellow stick like object protruding from the mud. Not really a stick but more of an umbrella, but Dave was not aware of such things.

There's no way I'm going to become stuck, he thought even though he was already waist deep in mud. His only chance was the strange yellow stick, but this was not quite in his reach. Dave knew that if he moved too vigorously the mud would take him and if he didn't the mud would still take him anyway. He made one final effort, thrusting one of his new arms towards the yellow stick. The goo sucked at his body, his arm shook with the effort as he strained and stretched trying to grab the stick.

Is this it? Is this to be my end? He thought. Suddenly the howling wind grew in intensity and the yellow stick wobbled further from his reach.

"Ohh nooo." Dave yelled in frustration, then "Oww that hurt."

A branch from a nearby tree had blown free in the wind and cracked him over the head on its journey across the muddied garden. His predicament had got worse. The bash on the bonce had hammered him further into the gooey mud. He was now up to his chest. The wind carried on blowing without a care.

HOWL, WHOOSH, WHOOSH, the wind continued, CRACK!

"Ow, ow… Ow, ow", went Dave. Yet another branch had been blown free and cracked him across his head. This time the branch had ended up in the mud next to him. He was about to pick it out of the mud and break it into little bits when a thought struck him.

"Ow." He said again. He had been struck with enough things already this evening, his head hadn't yet recovered from the branches and being struck by this thought was just the icing on the cake. As it turned out this was a good "Ow". He picked up the branch and holding it level he moved it around to hook the yellow thing's shaft, pulling it towards him.

Grabbing the stick and pulling himself slowly out of the mud he eventually got himself and his legs free. Immediately he leapt on to the yellow stick circling his arms and legs around it as he did so.

This is ideal, he thought.

Bending his knees and then stretching them again he managed to make the yellow stick move as if it was a pogo.

"Good." He felt the mud give way slightly. Holding the shaft of the yellow stick more firmly, to secure his position, he suddenly became unbalanced. His feet were thrown out from under him without any obvious reason. It was fortunate that he managed to still keep a firm grip on the shaft.

Whootompsch, went the yellow stick,

"Whooaah" went Dave.

The stick suddenly transformed itself; the bottom of the shaft had opened up into a coracle like object. Dave was now clear of the gooey mud and was standing in an up turned open yellow hemisphere. It was a bit like a ping pong ball that had been cut in half, about the size of the top of an upturned umbrella.

What an amazing piece of luck, Dave said to himself as he stared at the yellow material that was now between himself and the mud.

Bending his knees, once again, then leaping upward holding on to the shaft all the while, Dave managed to pogo the coracle towards the ramp of the hutch.

He was determined to get on the ramp and off the mud at the very least. With each jump he made he got nearer to the ramp and away from the sticky muddy goo at the end of the pen.

CHAPTER SEVEN

Tea Noises.

After bolting the door to his hutch Tariq went straight for the kettle and put it on. He really needed a cup of tea now to calm his nerves. He was happy that the whole episode of the peculiar weather and the strange landing of the banana thing had completed without further ado but something was still not right, not quite correct. After the kettle had boiled and while he was pouring his tea, a strange noise drifted into his ears.

Ssschlop, ftumch

This would not have normally been of any concern if it had just happened just the once, but it hadn't. Whilst pouring out his tea it had happened at least five times. In the beginning Tariq thought it was the tea bags moving around the tea pot. However when he had stopped pouring the tea and the noise 'Ssschlop ftumch' had continued. Tariq thought that may be it was nothing to do with the tea or the water he had used after all.

Being an individual that didn't really want to deal with any particular problem that wasn't strictly related to him Tariq continued drinking his tea.

With each gulp, gulp, that Tariq made as his tea went down,

Ssschlop, ftumch,

Ssschlop, ftumch,

Could be heard.

Tariq finished his tea and listened.

Ssschlop, ftumch,

Ssschlop, ftumch,

Tariq was now certain that this noise was not due to some kind of peculiar tea bag movement nor was it to do with his usual gastric functions.

Even when he got into his quilt and used the zip, which he had added, to zip the quilt up to his neck, he could still hear 'Ssschlop, ftumch. Ssschlop, ftumch'. Not a normal sound by anyone's measure.

To him it was definitely time to zip the quilt up across the top so he was completely sealed, thus avoiding any further need to investigate the strange noise.

Although I've had tea this does not seem to be the end of this peculiar evening… Tremendous, Tariq sighed miserably to himself.

CHAPTER EIGHT

Knock, knock, knocking.

Knock, knock, knock.

Tariq poked his head out of his quilt and looked towards the door.

Knock, knock, knock.

Tariq saw the door shake with the intensity of the knocking.

"Oh no." He sighed totally disheartened.

Knock, knock, knock

Tariq sealed himself into his quilt of invisibility. Not that the quilt was invisible itself. But he was sure that if he couldn't see it, whatever it was knocking at the door, then it couldn't see him.

This action was totally in line with his hastily formed plan to be disguised as a quilt so that, if and when, the knocking thing decided to enter he would not be noticed, in fact, he would be totally invisible, because the quilt camouflage would make him non-existent and when the thing entered it would take a quick glance around his hutch and say 'Oh! There's nothing here,' then leave bored stiff.

CHAPTER NINE

After Tea, Bed?

Dave knocked at the door for a third time. Nothing happened.

How am I going to get out of this abysmal weather? Dave thought. *Please let this door open… The weather out here is horrible.*

Dave focused his attention on the bolt that was fastening the door closed. A surprised frown crossed his brow. Could he believe what he was seeing?

If I slide this bolt sideways then, potentially, I would be able to get in.

Dave slid the bolt sideways and pulled the door open. He staggered into the hutch and as he looked around he instantly knew where to get some tea.

This is strange, he thought. *Where is the bod that showed me such kindness by giving me some dark eye apparel for this awful black wet evening?*

Dave continued to look around the room. He observed the tea pot, he observed the larder, and he observed the sleeping quarters. Nothing in his observation said to him that the hutch actually had a living occupant.

Dave was now very curious and a few questions instantly came to mind. *Who or what had given him, albeit in a very forceful manner, a decent pair of sun glasses? Who or what had left a yellow coracle for him so that he could get across the mud? And who or what had prepared the tea that was obviously ready for him to have a cup of?* Dave decided to ignore these questions and just go for the tea. He was particularly in need of refreshment. Dave poured out the tea and sat down in the nearest chair.

It was obvious to him that he had a few important things to think about. Sitting down and drinking tea was one way of starting to understand all that had happened. As he supped his tea he mulled over what had gone on. Dave looked around the room again. One thing was for sure, the bed, where he would have liked to lay down and rest did not seem to be a particularly comfortable place to rest. Looking at it, it struck him as very lumpy. There was a duvet, laid out across the bed, with a huge mound at its centre. Forgetting the lump in its middle the duvet was peculiar in its own right. It had a badly stitched on zip running along its side and around to its top. There was no real reason for him to be disconcerted about this apart from the fact that if he was to use this bed for the purposes of sleep the lump had to go. He had another sup of his tea and studied the bed.

Another question raised itself in his mind; *Why does this bed seem to be shaking?* Looking directly at it Dave could see that the covers could not be described as tranquil, furthermore, they could not even be viewed as remotely steady. He was definitely going off the idea of tucking down and sleeping on the bed.

I mean, Dave thought. *Who would want to sleep on a shaking bed?* It was only after this thought it occurred to him that a shaking bed was truly out of the norm and that something else must be going on.

He was not only in a hutch, but he was in a hutch that included the, all but impossible, shaking bed as well! Now there had to be a choice, a seat, or a vibrating bed. Dave concluded that in ordinary circumstances, the ones that he had been told about, a shaking bed could be quite intriguing; however, in this case, he was absolutely sure that there was something else going on.

Because of the fact he had had an extremely complicated evening so far, he decided he would finish his tea, before attempting to understand the shaking bed. Dave gulped the tea down.

Feeling refreshed he decided to seek out the ideal place to sleep. There was really no apparent place to sleep, apart from the lumpy bed; a lumpy and quivering bed at that. Considering all the options, i.e. bed or not bed, he decided to leap on to the quivering mass and determine where the buttons of the control unit were, so that he may turn off the quivering.

"Aarrgrahaa" yelped the bed.

"Aarrgrahaa" Dave responded.

"Yeowl" the bed carried on. Dave leapt off the bed and looked at it critically. The bed continued to shake and shiver. Dave frowned.

Why is it that whenever I try to do something normal it just doesn't work out right? He thought.

"Go away" said the bed, "You're not invited... you're not allowed in here." Dave did a double take and looked at the bed again.

"Who are you?..." Dave started.

"Go away", the bed re-stated firmly.

"No" said Dave even more firmly, "You are a bed and it is your purpose to provide adequate comfort for the provision of sleep for those of us who would like the choice of sleeping or not, as the case may be."

"OK. That may be so." the bed continued. "But, I am not a bed... I am a living being, one which deserves the space that I have claimed for the interior of my hutch, as it is my due!"

Understanding what the bed was saying Dave disagreed. "So in essence, you, as a duvet or bed, believe that you are the only one entitled to the horizontal position that you have attained and henceforth there shalt not be any other that wouldst partake of this positioning other than another duvet?"

"No." said the bed.

"No?" queried Dave.

"No. It is entirely possible that a quilt or duvet or bed, as you may have it, may merely be a quilt or a duvet or a bed, and that the voice of the bed maybe some other voice of a being not yet perceived at this moment!". Tariq responded. He was now seriously wondering whether he could come out on top of this conversation.

Dave considered what had been said.

"OK...show yourself".

Tariq thought about the proposition. He knew that if this situation was not resolved, now, further consequences were, more likely than not, to be expected. Being the brave and heroic person Tariq was, he unzipped and threw off the cover.

"Aaaagrrrhhh" screamed Shell at the top of her voice trying not to smirk. Tariq collapsed on the floor, shocked into a dead faint.

CHAPTER TEN

Friends? Not Quite…

Dave put his feet up; perhaps he would get some rest after all. He dozed off.

For both Dave and Tariq this had been a very traumatic evening and both were very glad to be out of the weather.

After a few hours of snoring at each other Tariq's eyes slammed open whilst his brain tried to figure out what had gone on and where it had been. Tariq looked towards the chair and then it all came back to him.

"Who the hell are you?" Tariq demanded.

Dave open his eyes and said, "Dave, and I could ask you the very same question"

"OK…" Tariq continued, "You have forced your way into my house and now you're sitting here stating that you are Dave. Because of this, I suppose, I should be telling you that I am

Tariq, Tariq of the Insomniacs, actually Tariq the Gifted of the Insomniacs. In this light what is your full title?"

"Forced my way in did I? There was a bolt on the outside. I slid it sideways and the door opened". Dave was astounded at this accusation.

"Yes. But the outside bolt is only for my own use just in case I lock myself out! And what about the sign?"

"What sign?"

"The sign on the bolt that says 'For Tariq's Use Only'"

"There was no sign."

Tariq thought about this and then remembered that the sign was still on the bench in his workshop waiting to be repainted.

"And as I said before, what is your full title?" he continued, dismissing the matter.

"I'm Dave", and thinking quickly to himself he added, "I am Dave, seventh of two hundred and eighteen thousand, three hundred and ninety four". Dave expected that this was a pretty good guestimate of how many others were in his crowd just before he had been blown free.

"But most call me Dave for short."

Dave was not a presupposing individual nor wanted to be. In reality Dave did not have any title but he just wanted to make Tariq, the Gifted of the Insomniacs, feel comfortable and if titles were the way then so be it.

This answer was not quite what Tariq was angling for but it would do.

"Thank you for letting me in." Dave added.

Tariq's chin hit the ground. "Letting you in?... Well Mr. Dave Foreshort, I don't think I had any choice did I?"

"Yes and No", said Dave

"Yes and No?" Tariq repeated, "Did I really have a choice?"

"Yes", Dave finished.

"And how is that then?" Tariq said all the more put out.

"You provided me with the things I needed to get across the goo and in doing so you gave me the direction! Without planting the yellow coracle I would not have been able to make my way to this fine hutch"

Tariq went over the last half an hour in his mind to make sure that Dave's statement actually fitted with the evenings events. Apart from the coracle everything seemed to fit.

Coracle! Tariq thought to himself. *Coracle!* Tariq thought again. After a few more seconds he understood, *Oh... umbrella... Now I get it.*

Yes it was true that Tariq had left the umbrella, yes it was true that Tariq had left his hutch to venture out to see what was going on and yes it was true that in returning to the hutch he had turned the lights on so that he could make a cup of tea and it was also true that he had not put up the sign stating that the outside bolt was only for his own use in case of an emergency. All in all what Dave was saying was the truth.

"As you can probably understand", Dave started, "I mean you no harm and I expect that you mean me no harm. Especially as you deemed it necessary to give me some Ray-Bans as a present."

Tariq did not know what to make of this. He had never meant anyone any harm ever in his entire lifetime nor did he want to, unless he was defending that, which he believed, was right in the presence of wrong doing. This was not a wrong doing situation. Probably not a situation that required defending, but how could he have known this without being informed of it in the first place?

Being of the generous type Tariq said, "OK. I understand that you have had a particularly hard time this evening, and may well need rest. So I will allow you to stay here until you have recovered from your trauma."

"Thank you. Thank you ever so much Tariq. I will never forget this ever". Dave replied.

"Right. It's still the night, the weather is rubbish…You can stay until morning. After that you will have to find your own place. OK?"

"Many thanks be bestowed upon you Tariq." Dave offered.

"You feeble minded wally". Shell added.

"What?" said Dave.

"Nothing", said Tariq, "that was just Shell. Ignore her."

"OK".

"There is another quilt in the cupboard over there if you need one." Tariq continued. "But once it is morning I would prefer that you left."

"No probs there Tariq. It is not my purpose to frequent one place permanently. For I am the helper of all needful things and to do this I must travel."

What an uptight arrogant fool this Dave is. Tariq thought. *And what is it with the gloves and boots?*

CHAPTER ELEVEN

Strangers Separate.

The morning arrived and Dave awoke.

"Tariq, once more I must thank you for the consideration you have shown me. May it be given back to you five fold... at least."

"Pardon?" Tariq yelled. His muffled voice drifted out from behind a thick, dark brown curtain which was hanging at the back of his hutch.

"I said..." Dave started, "Where are you?" He finished. There was no response just a noise.

Domp, domp, domp, domp, domp. It was the sort of noise a tortoise might make travelling at a surprisingly brisk rate up some old wooden stairs from a cellar.

"Here." Tariq poked his head out from behind the curtain, "What did you say?"

"I said, thank you for your consideration, may you get it back five-fold and I'm leaving."

"OK Dave. Perhaps we'll meet again, I don't know where and I don't know when but I am sure we'll meet again some sunny day or perhaps a rainy day even. Who knows?"

"Thanks for everything Tariq; you've been a good person to me. Bye". With that Dave opened the door to the hutch and wandered out making sure to close and bolt the door behind him.

Well. Dave considered, *what a nice person.* Dave strolled down the ramp, looked for the exit to the pen and made for it.

Today is another day, he thought.

*Well,*Tariq thought,*What a strange person.*

CHAPTER TWELVE

Nobody Ignores Dave.

After leaving Tariq's pen Dave looked around, where would he go now? Hearing some intermittent low purring sounds somewhere off to the rear of Tariq's hutch Dave decided to go and investigate.

He walked down what seemed to be a dingy alleyway between a wooden fence and an extremely tall wall made of bricks. He ended up next to what he thought was some kind of thoroughfare. It consisted of two parallel tracks of grass, each including trees with a huge concrete path laid out between them, if it was concrete, if it was a path

Dave looked at his watch.

Great, he thought as he discovered that he did not possess one.

He sat down on a low wall to think about what he would do next and where he would go. Surely there must be someone in this strange new world that could make use of his talents.

Nobody walked by, and even when Dave looked up and raised his hand to wave hello; Nobody ignored him and carried on down the avenue as if Dave did not exist.

"Oh well" Dave sighed. With nothing else to do he decided to relax and just watch this whole new world, unfold in front of him; particularly as the weather had turned rather nice now that the sun had come out.

Dave took the Ray-Bans from his pocket and put them on.

CHAPTER THIRTEEN

A Child's Misery is Only Known to Them.

"No, you can't look for it now and anyway you should have put it away after you", the children's mother moaned at them. "How many times have I told you; you must put things away after you. I have not been put on this planet to do the clearing up after you. Is that understood?" the children's mother added.

Hannah and Josephine knew what their mother was talking about and they always tidied up after themselves but this was not their fault. They had got their school satchels ready the night before, ready for their after school tuition. They knew what they had to do as this was routine. Both of them had put their stuff on the 'Going out tomorrow evening for maths lessons' cupboard shelf after having a go on the PlayStation and before going to bed. Their mother's chiding was the last thing they expected when they got in from school. They both felt so miserable.

"What did you do with the stuff?" Hannah said to Josephine.

"Nothing" Josephine replied.

"You are always doing this. Trying to get us in trouble."

"No I'm not," Josephine said almost in tears.

"Well, where are they then?"

"I don't know. They were on the cupboard shelf."

Dave opened his eyes shaking off the memories of his past. What had brought him out of his daydream? Dave listened. Anxious voices were coming out of the upstairs window of the house across the road from him.

"Josephine," Hannah said, "I told you to put our stuff on the cupboard shelf."

"I did," moaned Josephine.

"Why isn't it there now then?"

"I don't know. Please don't be cross."

"Why don't you know?" Hannah said ignoring Josephine's pleas.

"You were there with me Jo. We both did it."

Hannah had to admit Jo was right but how would she calm down her mother? Hannah did not know.

"Have you girls sorted your books out yet?" their mother asked again.

"No." Hannah had to say.

"Right girls. You know I'm going to have to cancel this evening's maths lesson and do you know how much this is going to cost? I only pay for this to help you, you ungrateful pair".

Dave heard the whole conversation. He was not only uncomfortable at the sisters' plight but was also intrigued about how the situation had come to pass.

I'm going to do something about this, Dave thought.

CHAPTER FOURTEEN

Problems are Hard to Fix.

Dave made his way to number 42, the Avenue. He did not know how he was going to get into the house nor how he was going to fix the problem.

But in his heart of hearts he knew, not only that he would help, but he could help, in some way or another. It was only the how that was the problem, and this being the only problem, he felt sure it would resolve itself.

It took him almost the entire day to get across the thoroughfare to the house. Every time he took a step on to the concrete concourse, which lay between the two grass verges, huge metallic things growled passed him and stopped his progress. As each metallic thing passed he felt a force drawing him towards them into their wake, trying to suck him on to the concrete concourse and into the path of their circular discs of steel. It was only his strength and the long grass on the verges that enabled him to stop himself being dragged into their path.

This world was strange; these peculiar growling monsters were strange. The only difference between each of them, as far as he could tell, was their colour. They came in blues, browns, greens, blacks, actually Dave couldn't pick out a skin colour they didn't have. Each and every one of them was lifted above the ground by sets of circular black rubber with silvery bits in the centre. All had silvery pipes sticking out the back which produced a deep growl as they went by. And all of them got in his way or forced him to grab hold of anything he could just to save himself from being dragged on to the concourse.

To Dave this didn't matter as he was going to get to the house come what may. He was a determined individual.

I will make sure that this strange force, whatever it is, will never beat me again, Dave told himself. Again another growling thing passed him and sucked him off his feet.

After a lull in the traffic Dave got across the concourse and strolled up to the front door and stared at it agog. The door was huge, huger than any huge thing that he had come across before. If he was totally honest with himself this was the hugest thing he had ever encountered before…ever. Apart from the sky, he added as an after thought.

Looking at the ginormous door it became obvious that this was not the entrance he was going to be able to use. Next to the door was a side passage, a side passage leading to the back of the house.

Dave, being the decisive individual he was (now), decided to go for the side passage way to see if it lead to any other entrance that he could manage to use as an entrance. The passage way was dim due to the shadows created by the closely packed overhanging branches of trees and shrubs.

Dave felt more comfortable using the passageway as he felt he was less obvious than the usual individuals that probably used this alley. He was very conscious that he stuck out like a sore thumb, not because he was a sore thumb but because he was a feather, a unique one at that, having an interesting pair of boots and a very curious pair of gloves, as he did.

CHAPTER FIFTEEN

Pleasing One's Mother.

Hannah and Jo sat in their room just staring at each other. How were they going to make their mother happy? Neither of them knew. Neither of them knew how they had got into the situation in the first place. It was not their fault but, as usual, they got the blame and this time they could not sort it out.

Jo jumped off her bed. "Hannah…let's look in the cupboard again, we might just have not seen where the maths books were."

"OK Jo." Hannah said, hoping that everything was going to be alright but doubting it in her heart.

Jo made her way to the cupboard with Hannah trailing. They were now both standing in front of the cupboard. Hannah reached for the cupboard door and pulled sharply on the handle. The cupboard door flew open and they stared in.

"Nope" said Hannah

"Nope" agreed Jo.

Nothing had changed. The shelf that they had put their maths stuff on was still empty. Jo burst into tears again.

"Hannah, how are we going to make mother happy? I have used up all my pocket money and don't have any left to pay for more books," she sobbed.

"Neither do I", said Hannah miserably.

CHAPTER SIXTEEN

Journey of Discovery.

Dave turned right at the end of the passage way. The rear of the property, which was now on his left as he had turned around, overlooked a fairly long garden that started with a broken down garden shed leaning against a broken down fence that ran the length of the garden and ended in an unkempt vegetable patch.

On his right was another seemingly impossible entrance type thing, but this one was slightly different. This entrance had a small square hole at the bottom covered with some kind of see through material which was flapping in the light breeze.

OK this is it, Dave thought, *this is my way to get in.*

Dave jumped up on to the back step and reaching forward he pushed the flap open, then let it close again. Dave's heart was thumping; this was sooo something that he had never ever done before and he doubted that any of his kind had done this before. That said, he still had a mission to accomplish, and accomplish it he would.

Pushing the flap open once more he pulled himself up into the gap and fell straight into the house. Dave got up and looked around, not seeing much because of his Ray-Ban sun glasses so he took them off and put them into his pocket. He looked around again.

Ah! That's better, he thought, on either side of him were many more doors, but they were much smaller. He decided not to investigate these but to carry on deeper into the house.

Leaving the room of many doors, albeit small ones, he entered a corridor. It was time to make another decision; there was an exit to his left or straight on along the corridor. Because Dave was not so sure he truly knew his left from his right, mainly because it was only recently that he had acquired arms, he thought it was best to carry straight on. So he did.

At the end of the corridor he came across another huge entrance that looked exactly the same as the huge entrance he had seen from the front of the house, on the outside, but this time its crafted contours were inset, totally opposite to what he had viewed from the outside. Behind him lay a huge cliff like cliff of wood and carpet, it consisted of regular short, flat and upright risers connected by similarly short and flat horizontal bits.

In his minds eye he could see the open window he had looked up at whilst sitting on the wall the far side of the concrete track.

Dave knew he had to climb this peculiar, regular, cliff face to get to where he needed to go. In achieving this he would be able to start his investigation into the problems of the children he had heard, the problems that had drifted down from the upstairs window earlier on.

Up the peculiar cliff he went. Getting to the top was a hard slog but being Dave he had managed it.

Arriving at the top he had three options, left, forward or right. Still not being certain of his left or right, he stopped and started using his nose, he sniffed. Smelling the air he recognised from the outside he turned to his right and strolled into the room he had heard the children's worrying come from.

Directly in front of him was a bed with two young girls sitting on it. They were each looking at the other in such a lost way that his heart went out to them.

Dave knew then that he had got to the right place. Dave also knew that the job he had to undertake was not going to be easy.

Without warning the children's mother's voice cut through the air. Dave shuddered.

"Girls…come here now. We're going out."

Dave dived, as fast as he could, behind the low chest of drawers on his left, (not that he knew it was his left for definite but for the purposes of this story it was clear!).

Both girls walked passed him, heads hung low, towards and then down the stairs. Suddenly there was a huge bang followed by a growl which Dave now associated with the metallic things that ran about on tracks of concrete using circular rubber circle things. Dave was now alone, or so he thought!

Now, Dave said to himself, *let's see what the problem is.*

He wandered around the room, looking high, looking low, and looking side to side.

"Oh gruntbuggerly." He swore. It was becoming apparent to Dave that he didn't have a feathers chance in a tornado to work out or even determine any way he could resolve the problem.

Some detective I'm turning out to be, some helper of needful people I am, Dave chided himself.

He sat down on the floor next to the kid's bed looking at the carpet for inspiration and started to ponder.

There was a sudden movement across the room; a CD flew by seemingly propelled by nothing.

Dave missed the flying CD incident as he was still staring at the floor in desperation.

How was he ever going to cheer up the kids by sorting out their problem? Did happiness come from being able to go to maths lessons? He felt it did in this case. Was he right to get involved? Yes, because it was his destiny to be the helper of needful people. Did he have any clue about what to do next? No.

That's an interesting bit of fluff, thought Dave as he continued staring at the carpet, *I wonder why it's blue?*

CHAPTER SEVENTEEN

Poltergeists? Don't Be Stupid.

The Movitall was having a good day. Yesterday was pretty successful as it had not been discovered whilst moving all those maths books and today was going to be just the same.

All the occupants of the house had gone out and the Movitall was free to shift other stuff without being interrupted in any way. Not even the damned rag bag cat, which was mooching about the day before, had protested enough to raise the alarm. But knowing cats was that unusual? The Movitall didn't think so.

It was very certain that soon, after these tests, the tests that it would have to pass, it would achieve fully fledged poltergeistdom and then be allowed to haunt any house that it wished to, for a small fee.

The Movitall made its way to the eldest kid's bed and heaved the duvet off, throwing it up into the air just to let it fall to the floor. As the duvet flomped its way towards the floor it puffed the dust and fluff around.

CHAPTER EIGHTEEN

The Makings of a Hero.

Dave had felt this sensation before; floating in air above the countryside, but when he looked down it wasn't the countryside he was looking at, it was just a carpet.

While he had been pondering, without realising it, he had become airborne. How could this be? He opened his eyes and saw the duvet lying crumpled on the floor. Floating about in the air was nothing unusual for Dave but suddenly being grappled by the intrusive hands of gravity was.

"Ooo that tickles", exclaimed Dave,

"Oh. Sorry", said Gravity in a low bass voice and adjusted its grip on him. Dave began making his way back towards the floor in a floaty fashion.

Gently drifting in the direction of the chest of drawers, where he had originally hid, he began to think that this floating was not quite right, especially as it had not been through his own choice.

However, perhaps it was normal, in the new world he had now become a part of, and him being of his kind.

As soon as he landed he jumped to his feet, bent his knees and held his hands out in front of him in the manner a karate expert wouldn't. Turning his head quickly in both directions he looked around the room, nothing… he could see nothing. There was no reason why the duvet would float up and then flop as all windows were closed, closed because the girls had shut them before they went out.

Next Dave saw one of the girls' pillows levitate itself and, with a determined effort, throw itself to the floor in just the same way the duvet had done.

These happenings were beyond Dave's normal areas of experience and to prevent himself losing any further concentration Dave quickly got back behind the chest of drawers. Once there he delved deep in his pocket for the Sterling Encyclopaedia of Unexplained Events. Thumbing rapidly through it he sought out 'levitating bedware'. To Dave's surprise and dismay the encyclopaedia stopped at 'bed' and continued with 'car'. No 'bedware' entry, levitating or otherwise, was to be found between 'bed' and 'car'.

Why Dave had made the decision to borrow this huge and heavy book from Tariq he had no idea. He also knew that it had been a totally pointless exercise. He put it back into his impossibly deep pocket.

CHAPTER NINETEEN

The Problem with Understanding the Problem is Understanding the Problem.

Wondering what to do now Dave decided to sit and observe until he had some kind of inspiration, just a little something that could get him closer to resolving the problem.

Not unsurprisingly another item in the girl's room objected to being stationary and lifted itself off the sideboard and migrated to one of the girl's beds. This time around it was the portable CD player.

Dave needed to get a better view of the comings and goings of usually inanimate objects. He thought that the top of the chest of drawers was probably the best place. He started to climb. Once at the top he was certain he would get a clear view of everything that was happening and once he did he would be able to decide on the particular course of action he should take.

Dave finally pulled himself on to the top and made his way to the middle of the chest of drawers. Stupidly he was looking about the room at all times trying to observe the cause of the movement of the girl's things and not taking any particular notice of where he was stepping. Directly in his path was an open pencil case with its contents, namely rulers, rubbers, superglue and pencils strewn across the chest top.

To his surprise he suddenly lost his balance as the pencil he had stepped upon skidded out from under his feet in a westerly direction. Cart wheeling his arms attempting to steady himself had no affect whatsoever. He sat down heavily on the tube of superglue which squirted its contents on to and under the pencil case. Being superglue it immediately stuck the pencil case to the top of the drawers.

Dave sighed with relief as he had just narrowly missed becoming a part of a sticky sculpture made from a pencil case and some of its contents.

I wonder how much I would get for that if I was an artist? He wondered. Dismissing the thought he carried on and sort refuge behind a jam jar which contained other writing bits and pieces. Once there he waited to see if any other events would unfold.

CHAPTER TWENTY

Exams can be Troublesome.

After the Movitall's success with the duvet, the CD, the CD player and the rest of the stuff, it was trying to figure out what it had to achieve next in order to pass the final tests that were expected of it.

"Well young Movitall", bellowed the voice of mystery from the netherworld. "You are on your final test and don't forget the four principles of otherworldliness that you will be judged upon".

"What are they then?", the Movitall said.

"The final test will be judged using the following criteria", continued the mystery voice from the netherworld.

"Damageeeee." It boomed with the word fading away in an echoy fashion until it was inaudible. "Styleeeee," the voice continued in its strange tailing off manner. "Controlll...lll, and aggression." Continuing further, "Damage will be judged upon how much of it you can inflict on the humans credibility, style will be judged upon the flare and panache used in doing the damage, control will be judged upon how you execute the style and finally the aggression will be judged upon how scarily you manage to achieve the previous three objectives", the voice finally finished.

The Movitall had managed moving and concealing the school books, it had moved a pillow; it had moved a duvet, a CD and a CD player, all of which were done impressively if the Movitall had anything to admit to itself.

What next? What next? The Movitall thought to itself.

Thinking back on its achievements with the school books, particularly as that had produced immense stress and misery in a certain few of the house's occupants, what could it do next? The duvet tactic had been a good demonstration as had been the CD and the CD player, but that hadn't nor would cause any particular strife.

So what next? If the school books were good then what else?... Ahhh, yes, the pencils and pens, actually everything that could be used to write. Now that must be the final choice, and in that choice the Movitall figured that it must achieve its best score yet.

Taking a deep breath the Movitall decided to go for the pencil case because without the books the kids could not do maths but without the pencil case and the pencils the kids would not be able to do anything at school. So they would not just miss one lesson they would miss the whole curriculum!

That's what I'm going for, the Movitall decided. The Movitall floated towards the pencil case.

CHAPTER TWENTY-ONE

Sideways Thinking.

Dave had been thinking, Dave had been fathoming and Dave had figured this,

If there is anything going on that I can not see, then what I'm looking for, must be invisible. Taking this thought a little further Dave continued thinking, *if what I'm looking for is invisible, then it must also be see-through, because that would make it invisible.* And continuing along that line of reasoning Dave thought,

To see through things you need a particular piece of equipment, something very special, something that allows you to see through things, something like X-Ray glasses perhaps?

However, the conversation in his head went on, *what I'm looking for is already invisible and that means I can see through it. So for me to be able to see the see-through thing, in other words, for me to see something I can't, I need at the very*

least some glasses that could un-see-through things that are see-through. Which can only mean, Dave thought excitedly, *that I need some un-X-Ray glasses! A pair of glasses that are absolutely normal in everyway.*

Dave put his hand into his pocket and reached for the Ray-Bans that Tariq had given him earlier. Putting on these ordinary glasses, these un-X-ray glasses, he was totally astounded at the result; the problem, all of a sudden, had become visible.

CHAPTER TWENTY-TWO

To Achieve One's Goal You Must Succeed.

The Movitall knew its goal. It floated towards the pencil case without a care. It knew that in moving the pencil case and placing it somewhere, it would achieve its highest goal, the one of maximum grief for the two girls. Not only would they not be able to do maths but they would not be able to do English or art or geography or anything. Apart from games, of course, which is not a bad thing, the Movitall continued thinking to itself, and wouldn't that be just great.

The girls would have to do games for morning lessons, games for mid-morning lessons, games for afternoon lessons, games all the time and all because they didn't have anything to write with or draw with. They may be able to get out of it once or twice with a note from their mother but that would be about it.

The Movitall swiftly patted itself on the back. This was it, this would be the final pass it required in order for it to achieve poltergeistdom. The Movitall was so happy. This was so simple.

Drawing itself up for the final pounce it lunged at the pencil case remembering the voice of mystery's words. Damage; well Movitall had certainly got that licked, style; Movitall did a quick loop the loop with a half twist finally bending its leg backwards and upwards at the knee, control; the Movitall just repeated the same movement only a lot more slowly, and aggression; the Movitall grinned in an extremely manic fashion whilst plucking its own eyes out with a pitch fork it had just materialised.

Cool, thought the Movitall.

Brave Dave

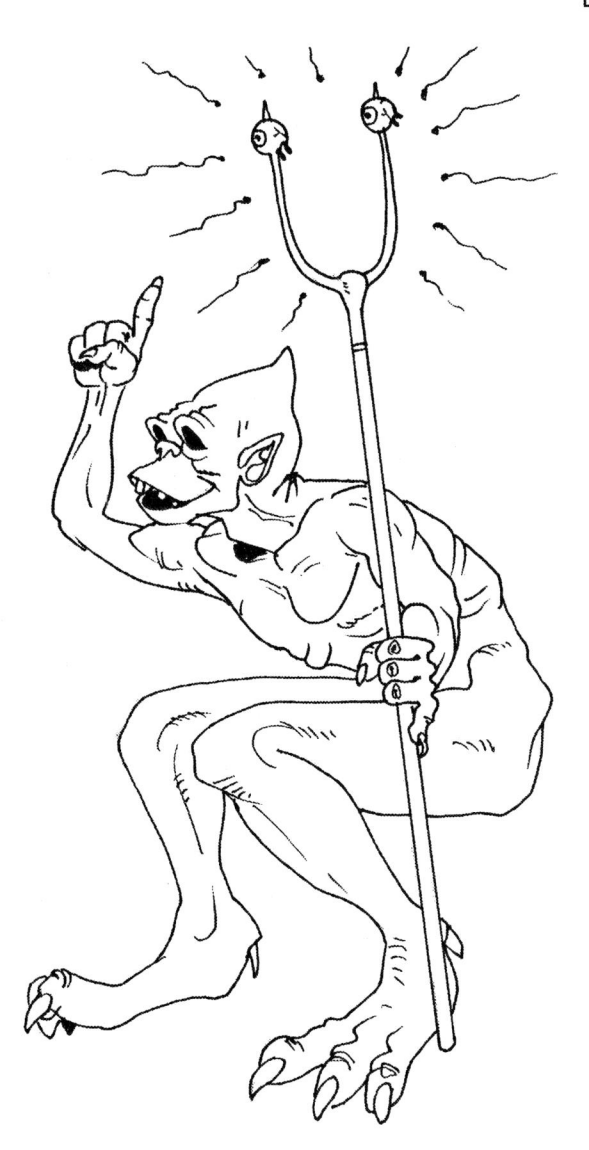

CHAPTER TWENTY-THREE

For the Want of an Unstuck Pencil Case.

Dave didn't know what to do, especially now, as he could see the cause of the problem that had been so harrowing for the girls.

Dave shuddered and quickly removed his Ray-Bans just in time to miss the pitch fork being buried into the thingamajig's eyes.

When the pencil case started to move violently backwards and forwards Dave slapped his un-X-ray glasses back on.

What he saw was the what-d'you-call-it puffing and panting, pulling and pushing and looking around wildly in a very worried manner. It seemed that the what-ever-it-was was not at all happy and all the while getting more and more desperate as the pencil case decided to stay exactly where it was.

"Ooohhhhhhh nnnooooo" wailed the Movitall in an omnipresent way.

"Ooohhhhhhh nnnooooo" wailed Dave shuddering as the Movitall's low and mournful moan vibrated through his body.

Deciding to play it safe Dave removed his Ray-Bans once more and promptly stuck his fingers in his ears, whilst peeking out from the corner of his eye, looking at the wobbling pencil case.

"No, no, no" the Movitall bellowed at the top of its voice. "This can not be happening, this can not be serious," the Movitall implored to no one in particular. It just didn't know what to do, what was wrong with the pencil case? How was he going to get his final pass? The Movitall stopped what it was doing and sat down heavily on the case.

Dave saw the pencil case stop wobbling and the top of it sink just as if something had sat on it. He removed his fingers from his ears and put the Ray-Bans back on. What he saw now was a very upset apparition sitting upon the pencil case leaning its chin into both hands muttering to itself.

Dave decided that he needed to hear what the apparition was saying so that he could further understand the current seriousness of the situation and to do this he had to be quite a lot closer to the muttering apparition than he currently was. He stepped quietly around the back of the jam jar then softly and slowly shuffled towards the CD rack which was behind the pencil case.

"What am I going to do now? What AM I going to do?" the Movitall continued to mutter to itself.

BING. A light bulb appeared from nowhere above the Movitall's head, in fact it had just been materialised there by the Movitall. It had had a new idea. The light bulb plinked out of existence only to be replaced by a puff of dissipating blue-grey swirling smoke.

Uh-huh, the Movitall said to itself, starting to smile at its new cunning plan.

Dave was getting nearer; once he had passed the CD rack and got behind the vase of tulips he would be right behind the thing and would be able to hear every single word that it muttered to itself. He continued to watch it intensely as he crept towards the vase of tulips. A frown of puzzlement leapt on to his eyebrows. The thing had now started doing, what only could be described as, squat thrusts; bending its knees, squatting down then stretching up and standing on tip toes. With each squat and thrust the Movitall sped up. Faster and faster it went.

Dave leaned out from behind the vase. He was soon to find out that this was a particularly bad idea.

The Movitall, with every squat, mumbled to itself, *I'm going to do it, I'm REALLY going to do it*.

The Movitall's new idea was based around using momentum. It thought that once it had built up enough speed then that speed and its weight, alone, ought to give it the ability to continue to execute any movement it decided to do without experiencing any resistance and it would then eventually be able to dislodge the awkward pencil case.

It had gone over every last part of its previous manoeuvre in its head. It analysed everything it had done to achieve the goal of grabbing the pencil case in order to move it to some other part of the house; a part of the house that no one would think to look in.

Just as it had done with the maths books, each and every one being rolled up and stuffed neatly down the centre of the unused toilet rolls in the bathroom, it would also move the pencil case to its allotted spot which was the bag of self raising flour in the kitchen. Obviously the whole point was not to get rid of the things it moved but just to place them somewhere where the humans would discover them later; somewhere where the misplaced items would be found. Found in a place exactly where they ought not to be; most definitely in the last place that any one of them would look. Maths books in the centre of unused toilet rolls, keys in the freezer, socks in the microwave, cat in the tumble dryer, dogs in next doors kids sandpit and pencil cases in bags of self raising flour, and so on and so on.

The Movitall had spent weeks remembering every place for every item. All of these places were detailed in the book that was central to a Movitall's education, a huge big yellow and black book called 'Poltergeistdom for Ghoulies'.

With two further squats and thrusts the Movitall made an almighty leap into the air. Up went the Movitall, moving extremely fast, causing a gap in the air where the Movitall had just been. The gap sucked other air into the void it had left and, unfortunately for Dave, it sucked him in to it as well.

Dave made a swift grab for the vase as he found himself in the process of levitating once again. Missing the vase completely Dave just about caught the top of one of the tulips, only for it to topple the vase and with it went the tulip, leaving Dave grasping at nothing. Dave was drawn upward in to some kind of uncontrolled vortex.

The vase toppled over and spilled its smelly watery contents on to the top of the chest of drawers, throwing the few stems of tulip that were in the vase across the chest's top and on to the floor in the process. Not much longer after that a puddle of slimy water spread across the chest top, a small part of which soaked into the prone pencil case loosening the glue as it did so.

"Whhhooaaahhhh", yelled Dave as he hurtled upwards, caught in the thingamajigs slip stream.

"Yea haaaaa", went the Movitall, sliding silently to a halt in the air as it prepared for its final run downwards towards the pencil case.

Zoom. Off went the Movitall.

"Aaaaagrraaahhh" the Movitall exclaimed suddenly as it noticed a strange brown feather wearing a look of horror and some silly gloves, hurtling towards it at almost the same speed that it itself was hurtling towards the feather thing.

Movitall blinked twice and revised its observation, a strange brown feather wearing a look of horror, some silly gloves and a particularly nice pair of Ray-Ban shades!

Dave braced himself for the massive impact, certain of his imminent demise.

Oh well, Dave thought. *This certainly has been different from what I have been used to. More different than what I was used to before I left the crowd. How strange this last day has been. Shame I never got to meet Tariq again. I'm certain we could have had many adventures. And what a shame that I never actually found out what those growling things that travelled the concourse outside were. Oh well, I wonder what time it is?* Dave looked at his watch to make a note of the time, just so that he may avoid this particular time in his next life if he ever got one.

Excellent, he thought as he was reminded once again that he didn't have one. *Perhaps I ought to get a watch, but there's probably no point now.* He concluded.

All through his ponderings Dave hadn't actually noticed that he had completely passed through the apparition as it had screamed through the air towards him. Looking straight ahead Dave felt great relief, albeit for a very short amount of time. The apparition had apparently disappeared. The short amount of time was now over and Dave became aware that he had a more pressing problem. There was a large white flat, huge white expanse of white ceiling that he was very certain would not suddenly step aside all the while saying 'pass by me, it's my pleasure' nor was he going to be able to pass through it unless he was extremely lucky. Dave thought that he must have used up all of his luck by now.

He braced himself for a huge impact, once again, certain of his imminent demise.

Oh well, Dave thought to himself. *This seems very familiar*, he added finally.

CHAPTER TWENTY-FOUR

Moving Pencil Cases and Exam Failure.

After its initial shock the Movitall was quite pleased that the brown feather had not reduced his momentum, the momentum which was part of its final strategy to move the pencil case and gain its pass in the exam so that it could become one of the coveted few; a fully fledged poltergeist.

Onwards and downwards, it thought.

The Movitall was about to engage the pencil case in some extreme momentum powered mov-it-ture manoeuvre.

Grabbing tightly hold of the pencil case the Movitall allowed its body to pass through the top of the chest of drawers into the top drawer all the while holding on to the pencil case.

Now push, the Movitall commanded itself.

The Movitall came flying out through the chest top expecting to suddenly slow down as it kept its grip on the pencil case. This, to its amazement, did not happen.

What? The Movitall thought as the pencil case came away from the chest top throwing the Movitall into an uncontrolled airborne somersault. The water from the vase had caused the glue to unstick temporarily.

"Whooaaaa." The Movitall exclaimed as it went spinning off into the air just like a raw egg would if it had been thrown.

The Movitall smashed clumsily into the light fitting which was dangling from the ceiling, still holding on to the pencil case.

The pencil case's sudden and unexpected release from the top of the chest of drawers had made the Movitall lose concentration just enough for it to not think about making itself less solid in order to pass easily through the light shade. The impact into the light stopped the Movitall in its tracks just enough to allow gravity to grab hold.

"It's alright", Gravity consoled glad to capture another victim, "I've got you!"

"Oh no" the Movitall groaned as it started an unwanted journey towards the floor. The Movitall was now falling with its back to the floor, the pencil case above it and its hand firmly stuck to the case as the superglue had re-hardened since the pencil case's release from of the chest top and the sloppy water.

As the Movitall tried desperately to remove its hands from the pencil case its flight towards the floor became more and more ungamely.

Bomp went the Movitall as it hit the floor.

"Flerr" exhaled the Movitall as the pencil case landed on its stomach.

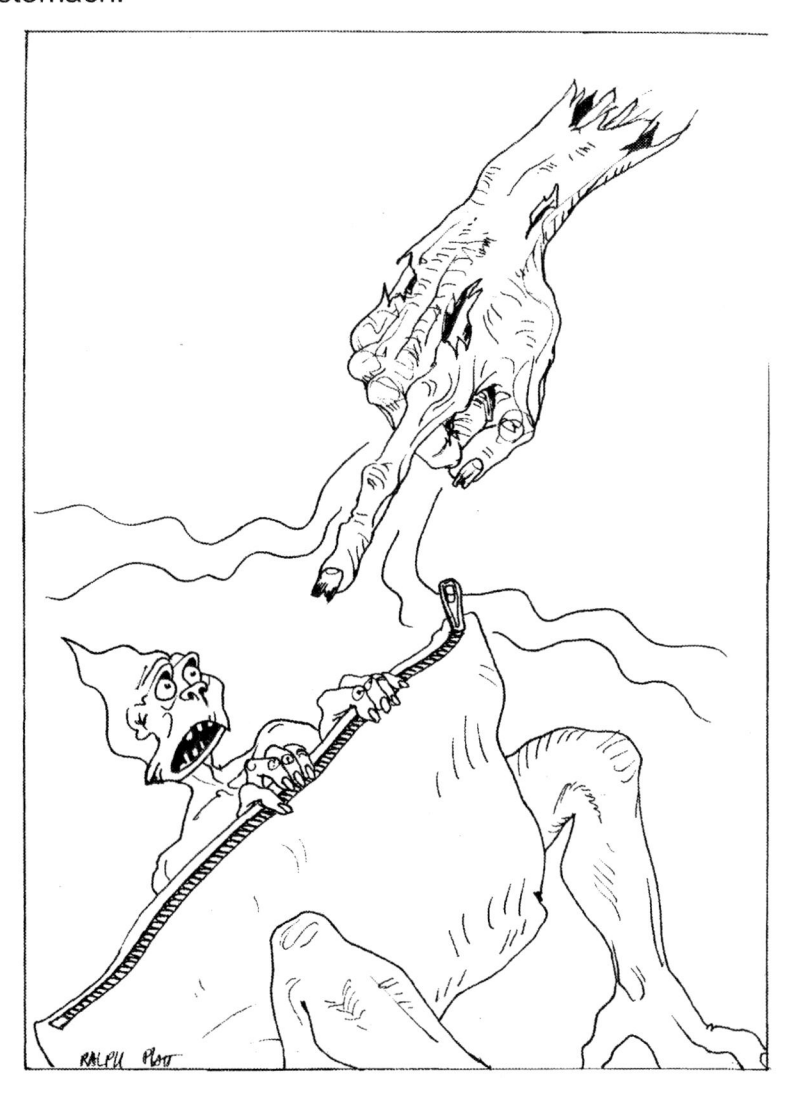

"Damage, style, control and aggression?" queried the voice of mystery from the netherworld. "Never have I seen such a complete and utter pigs ear made of the four highly held principles, principles that would have entitled you to become a fully fledged poltergeist, never. You have failed." voice of mystery concluded.

"No, no...", Movitall wailed. "No?" Movitall added finally, hoping the last 'no' would change the outcome.

"Never in all my death have I ever seen such a shambles be conducted in the execution of the four principles. Your time is over." Mystery voice said ominously.

"But, but, but," the Movitall said trying to think of a good reason why it should get a second chance. "It wasn't my fault." Movitall finished.

"Not your fault? And how so is that?" Voice boomed angrily at the Movitall's impertinence. "Was it not you that grabbed the pencil case?"

This was a difficult one for the Movitall to counter, especially as it still had not been able to detach the pencil case from its hands.

"No... I didn't expect you to have an answer". Voice of the netherworld said. "What has been done shall be undone. For failure is not tolerated nor shall the evidence of failure remain to be seen".

A thin rotting green hand with sharp and dirty black fingernails appeared in the air pointing towards the shaking Movitall.

"From here you shall be gone." The voice boomed.

"Nnnnoooooooo", the Movitall screamed in horror

A pus-yellow coloured light leapt from the end of the index finger on the floaty hand of horror and zapped towards the Movitall.

"Aaarrrghhh", screamed the Movitall shutting its eyes as its very being was reduced, first to a globby mass and then into a pile of dust finally dissolving away to nothing.

The pencil case twitched, then shivered, then leapt back to where it had started from. The maths books popped out of the unused toilet rolls, unfurled themselves and flapped gracefully from the bathroom back to the shelf in the cupboard where they had been quite happy until the thing had moved them. The duvet stood up, dusted itself down and flomped back on to the bed; pillow retraced its steps and finally the CD player burst into a few bars of 'Bat out of Hell' by Meatloaf, and zoomed back to the chest of drawers.

The hand then seemed to take an infinite breath inwards, shrinking all the while until it shloped out of existence.

"Aaarrggghhh", the Movitall screamed again as it opened its eyes only to realise it had been sent back to the first class of its last year of poltergeist university.

"No, no, no", the Movitall continued. "This is purgatory."

"Exactly", said the voice of mystery smiling to itself.

CHAPTER TWENTY-FIVE

Coracles Are Best.

With the ceiling getting so much nearer Dave had almost given up hope. He then remembered the coracle, he plunged his hand into his pocket and extracted the bright yellow pointy thing and pressed the button on its side.

FWOP. The umbrella opened towards the ceiling.

Dave's speed reduced. The ceiling started to stop coming so near, so fast. Then within the blink of an eye Dave started to float back towards the floor, the ceiling all the while moving away from him.

Well I'll be, Dave thought, *well done Tariq… again.*

Yet another item that Tariq had given him had saved the day.

CHAPTER TWENTY-SIX

All's Well That Starts Badly.

GROWL, CLUMP, CRAM.

Dave heard one of the multicoloured growling monsters pull up outside the house, the children and their mother getting out of it shutting the car door after them and then finally shutting the front door. The family were back.

"...and if you ever try that again I will not be happy." The girl's mother finished.

Hannah and Josephine ran up the stairs to their bedroom.

Dave had managed to get back to the floor of the room, fold up his coracle and shove it back into his pocket and sneak back behind the chest of drawers.

"How are we going to go to the next maths lesson without our books Han?" Jo said.

"Jo, we can't go without them and that is all there is to it"

"What can we do? Mother expects us to go to the next one because she has paid."

"I know Jo. But without any pocket money we are just going to get into more trouble."

"Han, did you really, really, really look properly in the cupboard?"

"Jo, you know I did. You were with me."

"I know Han, but we didn't do anything. Our books just went."

"Books don't just go. We must have just forgotten where we put them, that's all"

"But I don't remember us putting them anywhere else Han." Jo was even more miserable than before. "What are we going to do? We just can't afford new ones and Grandma won't give us the money." Jo continued

Hoping beyond all hope Hannah said, "Perhaps if we look in the cupboard once more we might see them. It might be that we just didn't see them for looking last time."

"Do you think so Han?"

"Yeah." Hannah lied.

"Ok then. Let's have another look."

Jo and Hannah went to the cupboard and stood beside it not wanting to have a look, a look that would prove they were still in terrible trouble. Hannah pulled the cupboard door open once more, slowly this time with her eyes shut.

"Hannah, Hannah, Hannah." Jo exclaimed jumping up and down, "They're there. The books are there."

Hannah opened her eyes, thinking Jo was not seeing the truth of the matter. But to Hannah's surprise there they were just as they had left them the day before. Hannah shut the door and opened it again, just to make sure. The books, the maths books were there!

"Yes Jo, the books are there," Hannah said not knowing what to think.

They were saved. It was then that Hannah noticed the vase on its side and the tulips scattered across the floor.

"Jo we'd better clean up the mess that Slime made before mother comes up."

Jo looked at the chest of drawers then at the floor.

"That stupid cat" said Jo.

While the girls got the cleaning cloth Dave edged his way out of the room and made for the regular cliff that he had gone up earlier. Down the stairs he went hoping that there would not be any more extraordinary forces that would make him levitate until he got out of the house.

The girls' mother was busying herself with some things in the room at the bottom of the stairs and Dave was able to make his way out of the house, back the way he had come.

He pushed the flap in the kitchen door open and jumped through it. He was out. Dave quickly made his way to the side passage and crept up it.

He was pleased, the girls were now OK and although he hadn't resolved the problem directly he felt, with some satisfaction, that he had been part of the solution, and how good was that?

CHAPTER TWENTY-SEVEN

Back to the Beginning.

Once back on the causeway Dave relaxed. He was still feeling quite pleased with himself. What could he do now?

"I know, I'll go and see Tariq and thank him for all his help". Dave was certain that without the stuff Tariq had given him he would not have been able to accomplish what he had. He felt compelled to thank Tariq. Perhaps Tariq would be interested in what had happened.

Only one problem now and that was how he would get across the causeway without issue?

However it was not a problem, darkness was settling once again and the amount of traffic was considerably less. Dave found it a lot easier to cross the concrete causeway and once he had done it he made his way back to Tariq's place.

ABOUT THE AUTHOR

Simon Woodward lives in Benfleet in Essex. He wanted to write a story for children that would cross over and be entertainment for adults also. The idea for a pseudo-super hero came about when he realised that you didn't really need to have any particular skill to achieve something, just the want to do so.

Before thinking that writing could be another avenue for his life's goals, he assumed that his job was the only thing that he was good at.

Through his wife's encouragement, Simon Woodward took up evening classes in creative writing and found that this new life skill was something that he really enjoyed.

"You don't know until you try." Is now his motto, and he applies it with vigour to every challenge that is presented to him. Some things don't work, but in the main it's fun finding out, he says.

He is now considering hang gliding and the only challenge there, is convincing his wife.

Printed in the United Kingdom
by Lightning Source UK Ltd.
119125UK00002B/118-171